Richard Whately

Historic Doubts Relative to Napoleon Buonaparte

Richard Whately

Historic Doubts Relative to Napoleon Buonaparte

ISBN/EAN: 9783337349844

Printed in Europe, USA, Canada, Australia, Japan

Cover: Foto ©Andreas Hilbeck / pixelio.de

More available books at **www.hansebooks.com**

HISTORIC DOUBTS

RELATIVE TO

NAPOLEON BUONAPARTE.

Is not the same reason available in theology and in politics? . . . . . Will you follow
truth but to a certain point? — BURKE's *Vindication of Natural Society.*

The first author who stated fairly the connection between the evidence of testimony
and the evidence of experience, was Hume, in his ESSAY ON MIRACLES ; a work
abounding in maxims of great use in the conduct of life. — *Edinburgh Rev.* Sept. 1814.

FROM THE ELEVENTH LONDON EDITION.

ANDOVER:
WARREN F. DRAPER,
MAIN STREET.
1874.

ANDOVER:
STEREOTYPED BY WARREN F. DRAPER.

PREFACE.

SEVERAL of the readers of this little work have derived much amusement from the mistakes of others respecting its nature and object. It has been by some represented as a serious attempt to inculcate universal scepticism; while others have considered it as a jeu d'esprit, etc. The author does not, however, design to entertain his readers with accounts of the mistakes which have arisen respecting it; because many of them, he is convinced, would be received with incredulity; and he could not, without an indelicate exposure of individuals, verify his anecdotes.

But some sensible readers have complained of the difficulty of determining *what* they are to believe. Of the existence of Buonaparte, indeed, they remained fully convinced; nor, if it were left doubtful, would any important results ensue; but if they can give no *satisfactory reason* for their conviction, how can they know, it is asked, that they may not be mistaken as to other points of greater consequence, on which they are no less fully convinced, but on which all men are *not* agreed? The author has accordingly been solicited to endeavor to frame some canons which may furnish a standard for determining what evidence is to be received.

This he conceives to be impracticable, except to that extent to which it is accomplished by a sound system of logic; including under that title a portion — that which relates to the "laws of evidence"— of what is sometimes treated of under the head of "rhetoric." But the full and complete accomplishment of such an object would confer on man the unattainable attribute of infallibility.

But the difficulty complained of, he conceives to arise, in many instances, from men's *misstating the grounds of their own conviction.* They are convinced, indeed, and perhaps with very sufficient reasons; but they imagine this reason to be a different one from what it is. The evidence to which they have assented is applied to their minds in a different manner from that in which they believe it is — and suppose it ought to be — applied. And when challenged to defend and justify their own belief, they feel at a loss, because they are attempting to maintain a position which is not in fact that in which their force lies.

For a development of the nature, the consequences, and the remedies of this mistake, the reader is referred to "Hinds on Inspiration," pp. 30-46. If such a development is to be found in any earlier works, the author of the following pages at least has never chanced to meet with any attempt of the kind.[1]

It has been objected, again, by some persons of no great logical accuracy of thought, that as there would not be any *moral blame* imputable to one who should seriously disbelieve, or doubt, the existence of Buonaparte, so neither is a rejection of the Scripture histories to be considered as implying anything morally culpable.

[1] See Elements of Rhetoric, p. 1, ch. ii. § 4.

The same objection, such as it is, would apply equally to many of the parables of the New Testament. It might be said, for instance, that, as a woman who should decline taking the trouble of searching for her lost "piece of silver," or a merchant who should neglect making an advantageous purchase of a "goodly pearl," would be guilty of no moral wrong, it must follow that there is nothing morally wrong in neglecting to reclaim a lost sinner, or in rejecting the gospel, etc.

But any man of common sense readily perceives that the force of these parables consists in the circumstance that men do *not* usually show this carelessness about temporal goods; and, therefore, are guilty of gross and culpable *inconsistency* if they are comparatively careless about what is far more important.

So, also, in the present case. If any man's mind were so constituted as to reject the same evidence in *all* matters alike — if, for instance, he really doubted or disbelieved the existence of Buonaparte, and considered the Egyptian pyramids as fabulous, because, forsooth, he had no "experience" of the erection of such huge structures, and *had* experience of travellers telling huge lies, he would be regarded, perhaps, as very silly, or as insane, but not as morally culpable. But if (as is intimated in the concluding sentence of this work) a man is influenced in one case by objections which, in another case, he would deride, then he stands convicted of being unfairly biased by his prejudices.

It is only necessary to add, that as this work first appeared in the year 1819, many things are spoken of in the present tense to which the past would now be applicable.

1*

A Postscript was added to the third edition, which was published soon after the accounts of Bunaparte's death reached us ; and another at the time of the supposed removal of his remains. A third, in reference to more recent occurrences, was added to the ninth edition.

NAPOLEON BUONAPARTE.

LONG as the public attention has been occupied by the extraordinary personage from whose ambition we are supposed to have so narrowly escaped, the subject seems to have lost scarcely anything of its interest. We are still occupied in recounting the exploits, discussing the character, inquiring into the present situation, and even conjecturing as to the future prospects of Napoleon Buonaparte.

Nor is this at all to be wondered at, if we consider the very extraordinary nature of those exploits, and of that character; their greatness and extensive importance, as well as the unexampled strangeness of the events, and also that strong additional stimulant, the mysterious uncertainty that hangs over the character of the man. If it be doubtful whether any history (exclusive of such as is confessedly fabulous) ever attributed to its hero such a series of wonderful achievements compressed into so small a space of time, it is certain that to no one were ever assigned so many dissimilar characters.

It is true, indeed, that party prejudices have drawn a favorable and an unfavorable portrait of almost every eminent man; but amidst all the diversities of coloring, something of the same general outline is always distinguishable. And even the virtues in the one description bear some resemblance to the vices of another. Rashness, for instance, will be called courage, or courage rashness; heroic firmness and obstinate pride will correspond in the two opposite descriptions; and in some leading features both will agree. Neither the friends nor the enemies of Philip of Macedon, or of Julius Cæsar, ever questioned their COURAGE or their MILITARY SKILL.

With Buonaparte, however, it has been otherwise. This obscure Corsican adventurer, — a man, according to some, of extraordinary talents and courage, according to others, of very moderate abilities and a rank coward, — advanced rapidly in the French army, obtained a high command, gained a series of important victories, and, elated by success, embarked in an expedition against Egypt; which was planned and conducted, according to some, with the most consummate skill, according to others, with the utmost wildness and folly. He was unsuccessful, however; and, leaving the army of Egypt in a very distressed situation, he returned to France, and found the nation, or at least the army, so favorably disposed towards him, that he was enabled, with the utmost ease, to overthrow the existing government, and obtain for himself the supreme power; at first under the modest appellation of consul, but afterwards with the more sounding title of Emperor. While in possession of this power, he overthrew the most powerful coalitions of the other European States against him, and, though driven from the sea by the British fleet, overran nearly the whole continent, triumphant. Finishing a war, not unfrequently, in a single campaign, he entered the capitals of most of the hostile potentates, deposed and created kings at his pleasure, and appeared the virtual sovereign of the chief part of the continent, from the frontiers of Spain to those of Russia. Even those countries we find him invading with prodigious armies, defeating their forces, penetrating to their capitals, and threatening their total subjugation. But at Moscow his progress is stopped; a winter of unusual severity, coöperating with the efforts of the Russians, totally destroys his enormous host; and the German sovereigns throw off the yoke, and combine to oppose him. He raises another vast army, which is also ruined at Leipsic; and again another, with which, like a second Antæus, he for some time maintains himself in France; but is finally defeated, deposed, and banished to the island of Elba, of which the sovereignty is conferred on him. Thence he returns, in about nine months, at the head of six hundred men, to attempt the deposition of King Louis, who had been peaceably recalled; the French nation declare in his favor, and he is reinstated without a struggle. He raises another great army to oppose the allied powers, which is totally defeated at Waterloo. He is a second time deposed, surrenders to the British, and is placed in confinement at the island of St. Helena. Such is the outline of the eventful history presented to us; in the detail of which, however, there is almost every conceivable variety of statement; while the motives and conduct of the chief actor are involved in still greater doubt, and the subject of still more eager controversy.

In the midst of these controversies, the preliminary question, concerning the *existence* of this extraordinary personage, seems never to have occurred to any one as a matter of doubt; and to show even the smallest hesitation in admitting it, would probably be regarded as an excess of scepticism, on the ground that this' point has always been taken for granted by the disputants on all sides, being indeed implied by the very nature of their disputes.

But is it in fact found that *undisputed* points are always such as have been the most carefully examined as to the evidence on which they rest? — that facts or principles which are taken for granted, without controversy, as the common basis of opposite opinions, are always themselves established on sufficient grounds? On the contrary, is not any such fundamental point, from the very circumstance of its being taken for granted at once, and the attention drawn off to some other question, likely to be admitted on insufficient evidence, and the flaws in that evidence overlooked? Experience will teach us that such instances often occur. Witness the well-known anecdote of the Royal Society, to whom King Charles II. proposed as a question, whence it is that a vessel of water receives no addition of weight from a live fish being put into it, though it does if the fish be dead. Various solutions, of great ingenuity, were proposed, discussed, objected to, and defended; nor was it till they had been long bewildered in the inquiry, that it occurred to them to *try the experiment;* by which they at once ascertained that the phenomenon which they were striving to account for, — which was the acknowledged base and substratum, as it were, of their debates, — had no existence but in the invention of the witty monarch.[1]

Another instance of the same kind is so very remarkable that I cannot forbear mentioning it. It was objected to the system of Copernicus when it was first brought forward, that if the earth turned on its axis, as he represented, a stone dropped from the summit of a tower would not fall at the foot of it, but at a great distance to the west; *in the same manner as a stone dropped from the masthead of a ship in full sail does not fall at the foot of the mast, but towards the stern.* To this it was answered, that a stone, being a *part* of the earth, obeys the same laws, and moves with it; whereas, it is no part

---

[1] " A report is spread (says Voltaire in one of his works that there is in some country or other a giant as big as a mountain; and men presently fall to hot disputing concerning the precise length of his nose, the breadth of his thumb, and other particulars, and anathematize each other for heterodoxy of belief concerning them. In the midst of all, if some bold sceptic ventures to hint a doubt as to the existence of this giant, all are ready to join against him and tear him to pieces." This looks almost like a prophetic allegory relating to the gigantic Napoleon.

of the ship; of which, consequently, its motion is independent. This solution was admitted by some, but opposed by others, and the controversy went on with spirit; nor was it till *one hundred years* after the death of Copernicus that, the experiment being tried, it was ascertained that the stone thus dropped from the head of the mast *does* fall at the foot of it![1]

Let it be observed that I am not now impugning any one particular narrative; but merely showing generally, that what is *unquestioned* is not necessarily unquestionable; since men will often, at the very moment when they are accurately sifting the evidence of some disputed point, admit hastily, and on the most insufficient grounds, what they have been accustomed to see taken for granted.

The celebrated Hume[2] has pointed out, also, the readiness with which men believe, on very slight evidence, any story that pleases their imagination by its admirable and marvellous character. Such hasty credulity, however, as he well remarks, is utterly unworthy of a philosophical mind; which should rather suspend its judgment the more, in proportion to the strangeness of the account, and yield to none but the most decisive and unimpeachable proofs.

Let it, then, be allowed us, as is surely reasonable, just to inquire with respect to the extraordinary story I have been speaking of, on what evidence we believe it. We shall be told that it is *notorious;* that is, in plain English, it is very *much*

---

[1] Οὕτως ἀταλαίπωρος τοῖς πολλοῖς ἡ ζήτησις τῆς ἀληθείας, καὶ ἐπὶ τὰ ἕτοιμα μᾶλλον τρέπεται. Thucyd. b. 1. c. 20.

[2] " With what greediness are the miraculous accounts of travellers received, their descriptions of sea and land monsters, their relations of wonderful adventures, strange men, and uncouth manners!" — *Hume's Essay on Miracles*, p. 179, 12mo.; p. 185, 8vo. 1767; p. 117, 8vo. 1817.

N. B. — In order to give every possible facility of reference, three editions of Hume's Essays have been generally employed,— a 12mo. London, 1756, and two 8vo. editions.

talked about. But as the generality of those who talk about Buonaparte do not even pretend to speak from *their own authority*, but merely to repeat what they have casually heard, we cannot reckon them as in any degree witnesses ; but must allow ninety-nine hundredths of what we are told to be mere hearsay, which would not be at all the more worthy of credit even if it were repeated by ten times as many more. As for those who profess to have *personally known* Napoleon Buonaparte, and to have *themselves witnessed* his transactions, I write not for them ; *if any such there be*, who are inwardly conscious of the truth of all they relate, I have nothing to say to them, but to beg that they will be tolerant and charitable towards their neighbors, who have not the same means of ascertaining the truth, and who may well be excused for remaining doubtful about such extraordinary events, till most unanswerable proofs shall be adduced. " I would not have believed such a thing, if I had not seen it," is a common preface or appendix to a narrative of marvels ; and usually calls forth from an intelligent hearer the appropriate answer, " *No more will I.*"

Let us, however, endeavor to trace up some of this hearsay evidence as far towards its source as we are able. Most persons would refer to the *newspapers* as the authority from which their knowledge on the subject was derived ; so that, generally speaking, we may say it is on the testimony of the newspapers that men believe in the existence and exploits of Napoleon Buonaparte.

It is rather a remarkable circumstance, that it is common to hear Englishmen speak of the impudent fabrications of foreign newspapers, and express wonder that any one can be found to credit them ; while they conceive that, in this favored land, the liberty of the press is a sufficient security for veracity. It is true they often speak contemptuously of such " newspaper stories " as last but a short time ; indeed, they continually see them contradicted within a day or two in the same paper, or their falsity detected by some journal of an opposite party ; but still whatever is *long adhered to* and often *repeated*, especially if it also appear in *several different* papers (and this, though they notoriously copy from one another), is almost sure to be generally believed. Whence this high respect which is practically paid to newspaper authority? Do men think that because a witness has been perpetually detected in falsehood, he may therefore be the more safely believed whenever he is *not* detected? or does adherence to a story, and frequent repetition of it, render it the more credible? On the contrary, is it not a common remark in other cases, that a liar will generally stand to and reiterate what he has once said, merely because he *has* said it?

Let us, if possible, divest ourselves of this superstitious veneration for everything that appears " in print," and examine a little more systematically the evidence which is adduced.

I suppose it will not be denied, that the three following are among the most important points to be ascertained in deciding on the credibility of witnesses, — first, whether they have the means of gaining correct *information ;* secondly, whether they have any *interest* in concealing truth, or propagating falsehood ; and, thirdly, whether they *agree* in their testimony. Let us examine the present witnesses upon all these points.

First, what means have the editors of newspapers for gaining correct information? We know not, except from their own statements. Besides what is copied from other journals, foreign or British (which is usually more than three fourths of the news published),[1] they profess to refer to the authority of certain

<hr/>

[1] " Suppose a fact to be transmitted through twenty persons; the first communicating it to the second, the second to the third, etc., and let the probability of each testimony be expressed by nine tenths (that is, suppose that of ten re-

" private correspondents " abroad ; *who* these correspondents are, what means *they* have of obtaining information, or whether they exist at all, we have no way of ascertaining. We find ourselves in the condition of the Hindoos who are told by their priests that the earth stands on an elephant, and the elephant on a tortoise ; but are left to find out for themselves what the tortoise stands on, or whether it stands on anything at all.

So much for our clear knowledge of the means of *information* possessed by these witnesses; next for the grounds on which we are to calculate on their *veracity*.

Have they not a manifest interest in circulating the wonderful accounts of Napoleon Buonaparte and his achievements, whether true or false ? Few would read newspapers if they did not sometimes find wonderful or important news in them; and we may safely say that no subject was ever found so inexhaustibly interesting as the present.

It may be urged, however, that there are several adverse political parties, of which the various public prints are respectively the organs, and who would not fail to expose each other's fabrications.[1] Doubtless they would, if they could do so with-

ports made by each witness, nine only are true), then, at every time the story passes from one witness to another, the evidence is reduced to nine tenths of what it was before. Thus, after it has passed through the whole twenty, the evidence will be found to be less than one eighth." — *La Place, Essai Philosophique sur les Probabilités.*

That is, the chances for the fact thus attested being true, will be, according to this distinguished calculator, less than one in eight. Very few of the common newspaper stories, however, relating to foreign countries, could be traced, if the matter were carefully investigated, up to an actual eye-witness, even through twenty intermediate witnesses; and many of the steps of our ladder would, I fear, prove but rotten ; few of the reporters would deserve to have *one in ten* fixed as the proportion of their false accounts.

[1] "I did not mention the difficulty of detecting a falsehood in any private or even public history, at the time and place where it is said to happen ; much more where the scene is removed to ever so small a distance. . . . . . But the matter never comes to any issue, if trusted to the common method of altercation and debate and flying rumors." — *Hume's Essay on Miracles*, p. 195, 12mo.; pp. 200, 201, 8vo. 1767; p. 127, 8vo. 1817.

out at the same time exposing *their own ;* but identity of inter-
ests may induce a community of operations up to a certain
point. And let it be observed that the object of contention
between these rival parties is, *who* shall have the administration
of public affairs, the control of public expenditure, and the dis-
posal of places : the question, I say, is not, whether the people
shall be governed or not, but *by which-party* they shall be
governed ; not whether the taxes shall be paid or not, but
who shall *receive* them. Now it must be admitted, that Buonaparte is a political bugbear, most convenient to *any* administration. " If you do not adopt our measures and reject those
of our opponents, Buonaparte will be sure to prevail over you;
if you do not submit to the Government, at least under *our*
administration, this formidable enemy will take advantage of
your insubordination to conquer and enslave you. Pay your
taxes cheerfully, or the tremendous Buonaparte will take all
from you." Buonaparte, in short, was the burden of every
song ; his redoubted name was the charm which always succeeded in unloosing the purse-strings of the nation. And let
us not be too sure,[1] safe as we now think ourselves, that some
occasion may not occur for again producing on the stage so
useful a personage. It is not merely to naughty children in the
nursery that the threat of being "given to Buonaparte" has
proved effectual.

It is surely probable, therefore, that with an object substantially the same, all parties may have availed themselves of one
common instrument. It is not necessary to suppose that for
this purpose they secretly entered into a formal agreement ;
though, by the way, there are reports afloat, that the editors
of the *Courier* and *Morning Chronicle* hold amicable consulta-
tions as to the conduct of their public warfare : I will not take

---

[1] See the third Postscript appended to this edition.

upon me to say that this is incredible; but at any rate it is not necessary for the establishment of the probability I contend for. Neither, again, would I imply that *all* newspaper editors are utterers of forged stories, "knowing them to be forged;" most likely the great majority of them publish what they find in other papers with the same simplicity that their readers peruse it; and therefore, it must be observed, are not at all more proper than their readers to be cited as authorities.

Still it will be said, that unless we suppose a regularly preconcerted plan, we might at least expect to find great discrepancies in the accounts published. Though they might adopt the general outline of facts one from another, they would have to fill up the detail for themselves; and in this, therefore, we should meet with infinite and irreconcilable variety.

Now this is precisely the point I am tending to; for the fact exactly accords with the above supposition; the discordance and mutual contradictions of these witnesses being such as would alone throw a considerable shade of doubt over their testimony. It is not in minute circumstances alone that the discrepancy appears, such as might be expected to appear in a narrative substantially true; but in very great and leading transactions, and such as are very intimately connected with the supposed hero. For instance, it is by no means agreed whether Buonaparte led in person the celebrated charge over the bridge of Lodi (for *celebrated* it certainly is, as well as the siege of Troy, whether either event ever really took place or no), or was safe in the rear, while Augereau performed the exploit. The same doubt hangs over the charge of the French cavalry at Waterloo. The peasant Lacoste, who professed to have been Buonaparte's guide on the day of battle, and who earned a fortune by detailing over and over again to visitors all the particulars of what the great man said and did up to the moment of flight, — this same Lacoste has been suspected by others besides me of having never even been near the great man, and having fabricated the whole story for the sake of making a gain of the credulity of travellers. In the accounts that are extant of the battle itself, published by persons professing to have been present, the reader will find that there is a discrepancy of *three or four hours* as to the time when the battle began!—a battle, be it remembered, not fought with javelins and arrows, like those of the ancients, in which one part of a large army might be engaged, while a distant portion of the same army knew nothing of it, but a battle commencing (if indeed it were ever fought at all) with the *firing of cannon*, which would have announced pretty loudly what was going on

It is no less uncertain whether or no this strange personage poisoned in Egypt an hospital full of his own soldiers, and butchered in cold blood a garrison that had surrendered. But, not to multiply instances, the battle of Borodino, which is represented as one of the greatest ever fought, was unequivocally claimed as a victory by both parties; nor is the question decided at this day. We have official accounts on both sides, circumstantially detailed, in the names of supposed respectable persons, professing to have been present on the spot; yet totally irreconcilable. *Both* these accounts *may* be false; but since *one* of them *must* be false, that one (it is no matter *which*, we suppose) proves incontrovertibly this important maxim,— that *it is possible for a narrative—however circumstantial—however steadily maintained—however public and however im-portant the events it relates—however grave the authority on which it is published—to be nevertheless an entire fabrication!*

Many of the events which have been recorded were probably believed much the more readily and firmly from the apparent caution and hesitation with which they were at first published,—the vehement contradiction in our papers of many pretended French accounts,—and the abuse lavished upon

2*

them for falsehood, exaggeration, and gasconade. But is it not possible — is it not indeed perfectly natural? — that the publishers even of known falsehood should assume this cautious demeanor, and this abhorrence of exaggeration, in order the more easily to gain credit? Is it not also very possible that those who actually believed what they published, may have suspected mere *exaggeration* in stories which were entire *fictions?* Many men have that sort of simplicity, that they think themselves quite secure against being deceived, provided they believe only *part* of the story they hear, when perhaps the whole is equally false. So that perhaps these simple-hearted editors, who were so vehement against lying bulletins, and so wary in announcing their great news, were in the condition of a clown who thinks he has bought a great bargain of a Jew because he has beat down the price perhaps from a guinea to a crown, for some article that is not really worth a groat.

With respect to the *character* of Buonaparte, the dissonance is, if possible, still greater. According to some, he was a wise, humane, magnanimous hero; others paint him as a monster of cruelty, meanness, and perfidy: some, even of those who are most inveterate against him, speak very highly of his political and military ability; others place him on the very verge of insanity. But allowing that all this may be the coloring of party prejudice (which surely is allowing a great deal), there is one point to which such a solution will hardly apply, — if there be anything that can be clearly ascertained in history, one would think it must be the *personal courage* of a *military man;* yet here we are as much at a loss as ever; at the very same times, and on the same occasions, he is described by different writers as a man of undaunted intrepidity, and as an absolute poltroon.

What, then, are we to believe? If we are disposed to credit all that is told us, we must believe in the existence not only of one, but of two or three Buonapartes; if we admit nothing but what is well authenticated, we shall be compelled to doubt of the existence of any.[1]

It appears, then, that those on whose testimony the existence and actions of Buonaparte are generally believed, fail in ALL the most essential points on which the credibility of witnesses depends, — first we have no assurance that they have access to correct information; secondly, they have an apparent interest in propagating falsehood; and, thirdly, they palpably contradict each other in the most important points.

Another circumstance which throws additional suspicion on these tales is, that the Whig party, as they are called, — the warm advocates of liberty, and opposers of the encroachments of monarchical power, — have for some time past strenuously espoused the cause, and vindicated the character of Buonaparte, who is represented by all as having been, if not a tyrant, at least an absolute despot. One of the most forward in this cause is a gentleman who once stood foremost in holding up this very man to public execration, — who first published, and long maintained against popular incredulity, the accounts of his atrocities in Egypt. Now, that such a course should be adopted for party purposes, by those who are aware that the whole story is a fiction and the hero of it imaginary, seems not very incredible; but if they believed in the real existence of this despot, I cannot conceive how they could so forsake their principles as to advocate his cause and eulogize his character.

After all, it may be expected that many who perceive the force of these objections, will yet be loath to think it possible

---

1 We entertain a suspicion concerning any matter of fact " when the witnesses *contradict* each other; when they are of a *suspicious* charac er; when they have an *interest* in what they affirm." — *Hume's Essay on Miracles*, p. 172, 12mo.; p. 176, 8vo. 1767; p. 113, 8vo. 1817.

that they and the public at large can have been so long and so greatly imposed upon. And thus it is that the magnitude and boldness of a fraud becomes its best support; the millions who for so many ages have believed in Mahomet or Brahma, lean as it were on each other for support; and not having vigor of mind enough boldly to throw off vulgar prejudices, and dare be wiser than the multitude, persuade themselves that what so many have acknowledged must be true. But I call on those who boast their philosophical freedom of thought, and would fain tread in the steps of Hume and other inquirers of the like exalted and speculative genius, to follow up fairly and fully their own principles, and, throwing off the shackles of authority, to examine carefully the evidence of whatever is proposed to them before they admit its truth.

That even in this enlightened age, as it is called, a whole nation may be egregiously imposed upon, even in matters which intimately concern them, may be proved (if it has not been already proved) by the following instance: It was stated in the newspapers, that, a month after the battle of Trafalgar, an English officer who had been a prisoner of war, and was exchanged, returned to this country from France; and beginning to condole with his countrymen on the terrible *defeat* they had sustained, was infinitely astonished to learn that the battle of Trafalgar was a splendid victory: he had been assured, he said, that in that battle the English had been totally defeated; and the French were fully and universally persuaded that such was the fact. Now if this report of the belief of the French nation was *not* true, the British public were completely imposed upon; if it *was* true, then both nations were, at the same time, rejoicing in the event of the same battle, as a signal victory to themselves; and consequently one or other, at least, of these nations must have been the dupes of their Government; for if the battle was never fought at all, or was not decisive on either side, in that case *both* parties were deceived. This instance, I conceive, is absolutely demonstrative of the point in question.

" But what shall we say to the testimony of those many respectable persons who went to Plymouth, on purpose, and saw Buonaparte with their own eyes — must they not trust their senses?" I would not disparage either the eyesight or the veracity of these gentlemen. I am ready to allow that they went to Plymouth for the purpose of seeing Buonaparte; nay, more, that they actually rowed out into the harbor in a boat, and came alongside of a man-of-war, on whose deck they saw a man in a cocked hat, who, *they were told*, was Buonaparte. This is the utmost point to which their testimony goes; how they ascertained that this man in the cocked hat had gone through all the marvellous and romantic adventures with which we have so long been amused, we are not told. Did they perceive in his physiognomy his true name and authentic history? Truly this evidence is such as country people give one for a story of apparitions. If you discover any signs of incredulity, they triumphantly show the very house which the ghost haunted, the identical dark corner where it used to vanish, and perhaps even the tombstone of the person whose death it foretold. Jack Cade's nobility was supported by the same irresistible kind of evidence; having asserted that the eldest son of Edmond Mortimer, Earl of March, was stolen by a beggar-woman, " became a bricklayer when he came to age," and was the father of the supposed Jack Cade. One of his companions confirms the story by saying, " Sir, he made a chimney in my father's house, and the bricks are alive at this day to testify it; therefore deny it not."

Much of the same kind is the testimony of our brave countrymen, who are ready to produce the scars they received in fighting against this terrible Buonaparte. That they fought and were wounded, they may safely testify ; and probably they no less firmly *believe* what they were *told* respecting the cause in which they fought : it would have been a high breach of discipline to doubt it ; and they, I conceive, are men better skilled in handling a musket than in sifting evidence and detecting imposture. But I defy any one of them to come forward and declare, *on his own knowledge,* what was the cause in which he fought, — under whose commands the opposed generals acted, — and whether the person who issued those commands did really perform the mighty achievements we are told of.

Let those, then, who pretend to philosophical freedom of inquiry, — who scorn to rest their opinions on popular belief, and to shelter themselves under the example of the unthinking multitude, — consider carefully, each one for himself, what is the evidence, proposed to himself in particular, for the existence of such a person as Napoleon Buonaparte: I do not mean, whether there ever was a person bearing that *name,* for that is a question of no consequence ; but whether any such person ever performed all the wonderful things attributed to him ; — let him, then, weigh well the objections to that evidence (of which I have given but a hasty and imperfect sketch), and if he then finds it amount to anything *more* than a probability, I have only to congratulate him on his easy faith.

But the same testimony which would have great weight in establishing a thing intrinsically probable, will lose part of this weight in proportion as the matter attested is improbable ; and if adduced in support of anything that is at variance with uniform experience,[1] will be rejected at once by all sound reason-

---

[1] "That testimony itself derives all its force from experience, seems very certain. . . . . The first author, we believe, who stated fairly the connection between the evidence of testimony and the evidence of experience, was *Hume,* in his Essay on Miracles; a work. . . . . abounding in maxims of great use in the conduct of life." — *Edin. Review,* Sept. 1814, p. 828.

ers. Let us, then, consider what sort of a story it is that is
proposed to our acceptance. How grossly contradictory are
the reports of the different authorities, I have already remarked: but consider by itself the story told by any one of
them; it carries an air of fiction and romance on the very face
of it. All the events are great, and splendid, and marvellous;[1]
great armies, — great victories, — great frosts, — great reverses, — "hair-breadth 'scapes," — empires subverted in a
few days; everything happened in defiance of political calcu-
lations, and in opposition to the *experience* of past times; everything upon that grand scale so common in epic poetry, so
rare in real life; and thus calculated to strike the imagination
of the vulgar, and to remind the sober-thinking few of the
Arabian Nights. Every event, too, has that *roundness* and
completeness which is so characteristic of fiction; nothing is
done by halves; we have *complete* victories, — *total* over-
throws, — *entire* subversion of empires, — *perfect* reëstablish-
ments of them, — crowded upon us in rapid succession. To
enumerate the improbabilities of each of the several parts of
this history, would fill volumes; but they are so fresh in every
one's memory, that there is no need of such a detail. Let any
judicious man, not ignorant of history and of human nature,
revolve them in his mind, and consider how far they are con-
formable to experience,[2] our best and only sure guide. In
vain will he seek in history for something similar to this wonderful Buonaparte; "nought but himself can be his parallel."

---

[1] "Suppose, for instance, that the fact which the testimony endeavors to estab
lish partakes of the extraordinary and the marvellous; in that case, the evidence
resulting from the testimony receives a diminution, greater or less in proportion
as the fact is more or less unusual."— *Hume's Essay on Miracles*, p. 173, 12mo.;
p. 176, 8vo. 1767; p. 113, 8vo. 1817.

[2] "The ultimate standard by which we determine all disputes that may arise is
always derived from experience and observation."— *Hume's Essay on Miracles*,
p. 172, 12mo.; p. 175, 8vo. 1767; p. 112, 8vo. 1817.

Will the conquests of Alexander be compared with his ?
They were effected over a rabble of effeminate, undisciplined
barbarians; else his progress would hardly have been so rapid.
Witness his father, Philip, who was much longer occupied in
subduing the comparatively insignificant territory of the warlike
and civilized Greeks, notwithstanding their being divided into
numerous petty states, whose mutual jealousy enabled him to
contend with them separately. But the Greeks had never
made such progress in arts and arms as the great and powerful
states of Europe, which Buonaparte is represented as so
speedily overpowering. His empire has been compared to
the Roman. Mark the contrast: he gains in a few years that
dominion, or at least control, over Germany, wealthy, civilized,
and powerful, which the Romans, in the plenitude of their
power, could not obtain, during a struggle of as many centuries,
against the ignorant half-savages who then possessed it; of
whom Tacitus remarks, that, up to his own time, they had
been " triumphed over rather than conquered."

Another peculiar circumstance in the history of this extraordinary personage is, that when it is found convenient to repre-
sent him as defeated, — though he is by no means defeated by
halves, but involved in much more sudden and total ruin than
*the personages of real history usually meet with, — yet, if it is
thought fit he should be restored, it is done as quickly and
completely as if Merlin's rod had been employed. He enters
Russia with a prodigious army, which is totally ruined by an
unprecedented hard winter (everything relating to this man
is *prodigious* and *unprecedented*); yet in a few months we find
him intrusted with another great army in Germany, which is
also totally ruined at Leipsic; making, inclusive of the Egyptian, the third great army thus totally lost. Yet the French
are so good-natured as to furnish him with another, sufficient
to make a formidable stand in France. He is, however, *con-*

quered, and presented with the sovereignty of Elba (surely, by-the-by, some more *probable* way might have been found of disposing of him, till again wanted, than to place him thus on the very verge of his ancient dominions) ; thence he returns to France, where he is received with open arms, and enabled to lose a fifth great army, at Waterloo ; yet so eager were there people to be a sixth time led to destruction, that it was found necessary to confine *him* in an island some thousand miles off, and to quarter foreign troops upon *them,* lest they make an insurrection in his favor![1] Does any one believe all this, and yet refuse to believe a miracle ? Or, rather, what is this but a miracle? Is it not a violation of the laws of nature? for surely there are moral laws of nature as well as physical, which, though more liable to exceptions in this or that particular case, are no less *true as general rules* than the laws of matter, and therefore cannot be violated and contradicted *beyond a certain point,* without a miracle.[2]

[1] ῍Η θαύματα πολλά.

Καὶ πού τι καὶ βροτῶν φρένας

ΎΠΕΡ ΤΟΝ ᾽ΑΛΗΘΗ ΛΟΓΟΝ

Δεδειδαλμένοι ψεύδεσι ποικίλοις

᾽Εξαπατῶντι μῦθοι. — PIND. Olymp. 1.

[2] This doctrine, though hardly needing confirmation from authority, is supported by that of Hume; his eighth Essay is, throughout, an argument for the doctrine of "philosophical necessity," drawn entirely from the general uniformity observable in the course of nature with respect to the principles of *human conduct,* as well as those of the material universe; from which uniformity, he observes, it is that we are enabled, *in both cases,* to form our judgments by means of *experience;* and if, says he, " we would explode any forgery in history, we cannot make use of a more convincing argument, than to prove that the actions ascribed to any person are directly contrary to the course of nature. . . . . The veracity of Quintus Curtius is as suspicious when he describes the supernatural courage of Alexander, by which he was hurried on singly to attack multitudes, as when he describes his supernatural force and activity, by which he was able to resist them. So readily and universally do we acknowledge a *uniformity in human motives and actions as well as in the operations of body.*" — *Eighth Essay,* p. 131, 12mo.; p. 85, 8vo. 1817.

3

Nay, there is this additional circumstance which renders the contradiction of experience more glaring in this case than in that of the miraculous histories which ingenious sceptics have held up to contempt. All the advocates of miracles admit that they are rare exceptions to the course of nature; but contend that they must needs be so, on account of the rarity of those extraordinary *occasions* which are the *reason* of their being performed. " A miracle," they say, "does not happen every day, because a Revelation is not given every day." It would be foreign to the present purpose to seek for arguments against this answer; I leave it to those who are engaged in the controversy, to find a reply to it; but my present object is, to point out that this solution does not at all apply in the present

---

Accordingly, in the tenth Essay, his use of the term "miracle," after having called it a "transgression of a law of nature," plainly shows that he meant to include *human* nature: " no testimony," says he, " is sufficient to establish a miracle, unless the testimony be of such a nature that its falsehood would be more miraculous than the fact which it endeavors to establish." The term " prodigy " also (which he all along employs as synonymous with " miracle ") is applied to testimony, in the same manner, immediately after: " In the foregoing reasoning we have supposed. . . . . that the falsehood of that testimony would be a kind of *prodigy*." Now had he meant to confine the meaning of " miracle," and " prodigy," to a violation of the laws of *matter*, the epithet "*miraculous*," applied even thus hypothetically, to *false testimony*, would be as unmeaning as the epithets "green " or " square; " the only possible sense in which we can apply to it, even in imagination, the term "miraculous," is that of "highly improbable,"—" contrary to those laws of nature which respect human conduct; " and in this sense accordingly he uses the word in the very next sentence: " When any one tells me that he saw a dead man restored to life, I immediately consider with myself whether it be more *probable* that this person should either deceive or be deceived, or that the fact which he relates should really have happened. I weigh the one *miracle* against the other." — *Hume's Essay on Miracles*, pp. 176, 177, 12mo.; p. 182, 8vo. 1767; p. 115, 8vo. 1817.

See also a passage above quoted from the same Essay, where he speaks of " the *miraculous* accounts of travellers; " evidently using the word in this sense.

Perhaps it was superfluous to cite authority for applying the term " miracle " to whatever is " highly improbable; " but it is important to the students of Hume, to be fully aware that *he* uses those two expressions as synonymous; since otherwise they would mistake the meaning of that passage which he justly calls "a general maxim worthy of our attention."

case. Where is the peculiarity of the *occasion?* What sufficient *reason* is there for a series of events occurring in the
eighteenth and nineteenth centuries, which never took place
before? Was Europe at that period peculiarly weak, and in
a state of barbarism, that one man could achieve such conquests, and acquire such a vast empire? On the contrary, she
was flourishing in the height of strength and civilization. Can
the persevering attachment and blind devotedness of the
French to this man be accounted for by his being the descend-
ant of a long line of kings, whose race was hallowed by hered-
itary veneration? No: we are told he was a low-born usurper,
and not even a Frenchman! Is it that he was a good and kind
sovereign? He is represented not only as an imperious and
merciless despot, but as most wantonly careless of the lives of
his soldiers. Could the French army and people have failed
to hear from the wretched survivors of his supposed Russian
expedition, how they had left the corpses of above one hundred
thousand of their comrades bleaching on the snow-drifts of that
dismal country, whither his mad ambition had conducted him,
and where his selfish cowardice had deserted them? Wher-
ever we turn to seek for circumstances that may help to account for the events of this incredible story, we only meet with
such as aggravate its improbability.[1] Had it been told of some
distant country, at a remote period, we could not have told
what peculiar circumstances there might have been to render
probable what seems to us most strange; and yet in *that* case
every philosophical sceptic, every free-thinking speculator,
would instantly have rejected such a history as utterly un-

[1] "Events may be so extraordinary that they can hardly be established by
testimony. We would not give credit to a man who would affirm that he saw
a hundred dice thrown in the air, and that they all fell on the same faces." —
Edin. Review, Sept. 1814, p. 327.

Let it be observed, that the instance here given is *miraculous* in no other sense
than that of being highly *improbable*.

worthy of credit. What, for instance, would the great Hume, or any of the philosophers of his school, have said, if they had found, in the antique records of any nation, such a passage as this?—" There was a certain man of Corsica, whose name was Napoleon, and he was one of the chief captains of the host of the French; and he gathered together an army, and went and fought against Egypt; but when the king of Britain heard thereof, he sent ships of war and valiant men to fight against the French in Egypt. So they warred against them, and prevailed, and strengthened the hands of the rulers of the land against the French, and drave away Napoleon from before the city of Acre. Then Napoleon left the captains and the army that were in Egypt, and fled, and returned back to France. So the French people took Napoleon, and made him ruler over them, and he became exceeding great, insomuch as there was none like him of all that had ruled over France before."

What, I say, would Hume have thought of this, especially if he had been told that it was at this day generally credited? Would he not have confessed that he had been mistaken in supposing there was a peculiarly blind credulity and prejudice in favor of everything that is accounted *sacred;* [1] for that, since even professed sceptics swallow implicitly such a story as this, it appears there must be a still blinder prejudice in favor of everything that is *not* accounted sacred?

Suppose, again, we found in this history such passages as the following: "And it came to pass after these things that Napoleon strengthened himself, and gathered together another host instead of that which he had lost, and went and warred against the Prussians, and the Russians, and the Austrians,

---

[1] "If the spirit of religion join itself to the love of wonder, there is an end of common sense; and human testimony in these circumstances loses all pretensions to authority." — *Hume's Essay on Miracles*, p. 179, 12mo.; p. 185, 8vo. 1767; p. 117, 8vo. 1817.

and all the rulers of the north country, which were confederate against him. And the ruler of Sweden, also, which was a Frenchman, warred against Napoleon. So they went forth, and fought against the French in the plain of Leipsic. And the French were discomfited before their enemies, and fled and came to the rivers which are behind Leipsic, and essayed to pass over, that they might escape out of the hand of their enemies; but they could not; for Napoleon had broken down the bridges; so the people of the north countries came upon them, and smote them with a very grievous slaughter." . . . .

"Then the ruler of Austria and all the rulers of the north countries sent messengers unto Napoleon to speak peaceably unto him, saying, Why should there be war between us any more? Now Napoleon had put away his wife, and taken the daughter of the ruler of Austria to wife. So all the counsellors of Napoleon came and stood before him, and said, Behold now these kings are merciful kings; do even as they say unto thee; knowest thou not yet that France is destroyed? But he spake roughly unto his counsellors, and drave them out from his presence, neither would he hearken unto their voice. And when all the kings saw that, they warred against France, and smote it with the edge of the sword, and came near to Paris, which is the royal city, to take it: so the men of Paris went out, and delivered up the city to them. Then those kings spake kindly unto the men of Paris, saying, Be of good cheer, there shall no harm happen unto you. Then were the men of Paris glad, and said, Napoleon is a tyrant; he shall no more rule over us: also all the princes, the judges, the counsellors, and the captains whom Napoleon had raised up even from the lowest of the people, sent unto Lewis the brother of King Lewis, whom he had slain, and made him king over France." . . . .

"And when Napoleon saw that the kingdom was departed

3*

from him, he said unto the rulers which came against him,
Let me, I pray you, give the kingdom unto my son; but they
would not hearken unto him. Then he spake yet again, saying, Let me, I pray you, go and live in the island of Elba,
which is over against Italy, nigh unto the coast of France;
and ye shall give me an allowance for me and my household,
and the land of Elba also for a possession. So they made
him ruler of Elba.". . . .

" In those days the Pope returned unto his own land. Now
the French, and divers other nations of Europe, are servants
of the Pope, and hold him in reverence ; but he is an abom-
ination unto the Britons, and to the Prussians, and to the Russians, and to the Swedes. Howbeit, the French had taken
away all his lands, and robbed him of all that he had, and carried him away captive into France. But when the Britons,
and the Prussians, and the Russians, and the Swedes, and the
rest of the nations that were confederate against France, came
thither, they caused the French to set the Pope at liberty, and
to restore all his goods that they had taken ; likewise they
gave him back all his possessions ; and he went home in peace,
and ruled over his own city as in times past.". . . .

" And it came to pass when Napoleon had not yet been a
full year at Elba, that he said unto his men of war that clave
unto him, Go to, let us go back to France, and fight against
King Lewis, and thrust him out from being king. So he departed, he and six hundred men with him that drew the sword,
and warred against King Lewis. Then all the men of Belial
gathered themselves together, and said, God save Napoleon.
And when Lewis saw that, he fled, and gat him into the land
of Batavia ; and Napoleon ruled over France," etc. etc. etc.

Now if a free-thinking philosopher — one of those who advocate the cause of unbiased reason, and despise pretended
revelations — were to meet with such a tissue of absurdities as

this in an old Jewish record, would he not reject it at once as too palpable an imposture[1] to deserve even any inquiry into its evidence? Is that credible, then, of the civilized Europeans now, which could not, if reported of the semi-barbarous Jews three thousand years ago, be established by any testimony? Will it be answered, that " there is nothing *supernatural* in all this?" Why is it, then, that you object to what is *supernatural*—that you reject every account of *miracles*—if not because they are *improbable*? Surely, then, a story equally or still more improbable is not to be implicitly received merely on the ground that it is *not* miraculous; though in fact, as I have already (in note, p. 26) shown from Hume's authority, it really *is* miraculous. The opposition to experience has been proved to be as complete in this case as in what are commonly called miracles; and the reasons assigned for that contrariety by the defenders of *them*, cannot be pleaded in the present instance. If, then, philosophers who reject every wonderful story that is maintained by priests are yet found ready to believe *everything else*, however improbable, they will surely lay themselves open to the accusation brought against them of being unduly prejudiced against whatever relates to religion.

There is one more circumstance which I cannot forbear mentioning, because it so much adds to the air of fiction which pervades every part of this marvellous tale; and that is, the *nationality* of it.[2]

---

[1] " I desire any one to lay his hand upon his heart, and after serious consideration declare whether he thinks that the falsehood of such a book, supported by such testimony, would be more extraordinary and miraculous than all the miracles it relates."— *Hume's Essay on Miracles*, p. 200, 12mo.; p. 206, 8vo. 1767; p. 131, 8vo. 1817.

Let it be borne in mind, that Hume (as I have above remarked) continually employs the term " miracle " and " prodigy " to signify anything that is highly *improbable* and *extraordinary*.

[2] " The wise lend a very academic faith to every report which favors the pas-

Buonaparte prevailed over all the hostile states in turn, *except England;* in the zenith of his power, his fleets were swept from the sea *by England;* his troops always defeat an equal, and frequently even a superior number of those of any other nation, *except the English;* and with them it is just the reverse; twice, and twice only, he is personally engaged against an *English commander,* and both times he is totally defeated — at Acre and at Waterloo; and to crown all, *England* finally crushes this tremendous power, which had so long kept the continent in subjection or in alarm, and to the *English* he surrenders himself prisoner! Thoroughly national, to be sure! It *may* be all very true; but I would only ask, *if* a story *had* been fabricated for the express purpose of amusing the English nation, could it have been contrived more ingeniously? It would do admirably for an epic poem; and, indeed, bears a considerable resemblance to the Iliad and the Æneid, in which Achilles and the Greeks, Æneas and the Trojans (the ancestors of the Romans), are so studiously held up to admiration. Buonaparte's exploits seem magnified in order to enhance the glory of his conquerors, just as Hector is allowed to triumph during the absence of Achilles, merely to give additional splendor to his overthrow by the arm of that invincible hero. Would not this circumstance alone render a history rather *suspicious* in the eyes of an acute critic, even if it were not filled with such gross improbabilities, and induce him to suspend his judgment till very satisfactory evidence (far stronger than can be found in this case) should be produced?

Is it, then, too much to demand of the wary academic[1] a sus-

---

sion of the reporter, whether it magnifies his *country,* his family, or himself." — *Hume's Essay on Miracles,* p. 144, 12mo.; p. 200, 8vo. 1767; p. 126, 8vo. 1817.

[1] " Nothing can be more contrary than such a philosophy " (the academic or sceptical) " to the supine indolence of the mind, its rash arrogance, its lofty pre-

pension of judgment as to the "life and adventures of Napoleon Buonaparte?" I do no pretend to *decide* positively that there is not, nor ever was, any such person, but merely to propose it as a *doubtful* point, and one the more deserving of careful investigation from the very circumstance of its having hitherto been admitted without inquiry. Far less would I undertake to decide what is, or has been, the real state of affairs. He who points out the improbability of the current story is not bound to suggest an hypothesis of his own ;[1] though it may be safely affirmed that it would be hard to invent any one more improbable than the received one. One may surely be allowed to hesitate in admitting the stories which the ancient poets tell of earthquakes and volcanic eruptions being caused by imprisoned giants, without being called upon satisfactorily to account for those phenomena.

Amidst the defect of valid evidence under which, as I have already shown, we labor in the present instance, it is hardly possible to offer more than here and there a probable conjecture ; or to pronounce how much may be true, and how much fictitious, in the accounts presented to us. For it is to be observed that this case is much *more* open to sceptical doubts even than some miraculous histories ; for some of *them* are of such a nature that you cannot consistently admit a part and reject the rest, but are bound, if you are satisfied as to the reality of any one miracle, to embrace the whole system ; so that it is necessary for the sceptic to impeach the evidence of *all* of them, separately and collectively ; whereas *here* each single point requires to be *established* separately, since no one of them authenticates the rest. Supposing there be a state prisoner,

tensions, and its superstitious credulity."— *Fifth Essay*, p. 68, 12mo.; p. 41, 8vo. 1817.

[1] See Hume's Essay on Miracles, pp. 189, 191, 195, 12mo.; pp. 193, 197, 201, 202, 8vo. 1767; pp. 124, 125, 126, 8vo. 1817.

at St. Helena (which, by the way, it is acknowledged, many of the French disbelieve), how do we know who he is, or why he is confined there? There have been state prisoners, before now, who were never guilty of subjugating half Europe, and whose offences have been very imperfectly ascertained. Admitting that there have been bloody wars going on for several years past, which is highly probable, it does not follow that the events of those wars were such as we have been told that Buonaparte was the author and conductor of them; or that such a person ever existed. What disturbances may have taken place in the government of the French people, we, and even nineteen twentieths of *them*, have no means of learning but from imperfect hearsay evidence; and how much credit they themselves attach to that evidence is very doubtful. This at least is certain, — that a M. Berryer, a French advocate, has published memoirs, professing to record many of the recent events of the history of France, in which, among other things, he states his conviction that Buonaparte's escape from Elba was DESIGNED AND CONTRIVED BY THE ENGLISH GOVERN- MENT.[1] And we are assured by many travellers that this was, and is, commonly reported in France.

Now, that the French should believe the whole story about Buonaparte, according to this version of it, does seem utterly incredible. Let any one suppose them seriously believing that we maintained for many years a desperate struggle against this formidable emperor of theirs, in the course of which we expended such an enormous amount of blood and treasure as is reported; that we finally, after encountering enormous risks, succeeded in subduing him, and secured him in a place of safe exile; and that, in less than a year after, we turned him out again, like a bag-fox, or rather a bag-lion, for the sake of amusing ourselves by again staking all that was dear to us on

---

[1] See Edinburgh Review for October, 1842, p. 162.

the event of a doubtful and bloody battle, in which defeat must be ruinous, and victory, if obtained at all, must cost us many thousands of our best soldiers. Let any one force himself for a moment to conceive the French seriously believing such a mass of absurdity; and the inference must be that such a people must be prepared to believe anything. They might fancy their own country to abound not only with Napoleons, but with dragons and centaurs, and "men whose heads do grow beneath their shoulders," or anything else that any lunatic ever dreamed of. If we could suppose the French capable of such monstrous credulity as the above supposition would imply, it is plain their testimony must be altogether worthless.

But, on the other hand, suppose them to be aware that the British Government have been all along imposing on us, and it is quite natural that they should deride our credulity, and try whether there is anything too extravagant for us to swallow. And, indeed, if Buonaparte was in fact altogether a phantom conjured up by the British Ministers, then it is *true* that his escape from Elba really *was*, as well as *the rest of his exploits*, a contrivance of theirs.

But whatever may be believed by the French relative to the recent occurrences in their own country, and whatever may be the real character of these occurrences, of this, at least, we are well assured, that there have been numerous bloody wars with France under the dominion of the *Bourbons;* and we are now told that France is governed by a Bourbon king, of the name of Lewis, who professes to be in the twenty-third year of his reign. Let every one conjecture for himself. I am far from pretending to decide who may have been the governor or governors of the French nation, and the leaders of their armies, for several years past. Certain it is, that when men are indulging their inclination for the marvellous, they always

show a strong propensity to accumulate upon *one* individual
(real or imaginary) the exploits of many; besides multiplying
and exaggerating these exploits a thousand-fold. Thus, the
expounders of the ancient mythology tell us there were several
persons of the name of Hercules (either originally bearing
that appellation, or having it applied to them as an honor),
whose collective feats, after being dressed up in a sufficiently
marvellous garb, were attributed to a single hero. Is it not
just possible, that during the rage for words of Greek deriva-
tion, the title of "Napoleon" (Ναπολέων), which signifies "lion
of the forest," may have been conferred by the popular voice
on more than one favorite general, distinguished for irresistible
valor? Is it not also possible that "BUONA PARTE" may have
been originally a sort of cant term applied to the "good (that is,
the bravest, or most patriotic) part" of the French army, collectively, and have been afterwards mistaken for the proper
name of an individual?[1] I do not profess to support this conjecture; but it is certain that such mistakes may and do occur.
Some critics have supposed that the Athenians imagined AN-
ASTIS ("Resurrection") to be a new goddess, in whose cause
Paul was preaching. Would it have been thought anything
incredible if we had been told that the ancient Persians, who
had no idea of any but a monarchical government, had supposed

[1] It is well known with how much learning and ingenuity the Rationalists of
the German school have labored to throw discredit on the literal interpretation
of the narratives, both of the Old and New Testaments; representing them as
MYTHS, that is, fables allegorically describing some physical or moral phenomena — philosophical principles — systems, etc. — under the figure of actions
performed by certain ideal personages; these allegories having been, afterwards,
through the mistake of the vulgar, believed as history. Thus, the real historical
existence of such a person as the supposed founder of the Christian religion,
and the acts attributed to him, are denied in the literal sense, and the whole of
the evangelical history is explained on the "mythical" theory.

Now it is a remarkable circumstance, in reference to the point at present befc re
us, that an eminent authoress of this century has distinctly declared the Napoleon Buonaparte was NOT A MAN, but a SYSTEM.

Aristocratia to be a queen of Sparta? But we need not con-fine ourselves to hypothetical cases: it is positively stated that the Hindoos at this day believe " the honorable East India Company " to be a venerable old lady of high dignity, residing in this country. The Germans, again, of the present day de-rive their name from a similar mistake. The first tribe of them who invaded Gaul[1] assumed the honorable title of "*Ger-man*," which signifies " warriors " (the words " war " and " guerre," as well as " man," which remains in our language unaltered, are evidently derived from the Teutonic), and the Gauls ap-plied this as a *name* to the whole *race.*

However, I merely throw out these conjectures, without by any means contending that more plausible ones might not be suggested. But whatever supposition we adopt, or whether we adopt any, the objections to the commonly received accounts will remain in their full force, and imperiously demand the attention of the candid sceptic.

I call upon those, therefore, who profess themselves advocates of free inquiry, — who disdain to be carried along with the stream of popular opinion, and who will listen to no testimony that runs counter to experience, — to follow up their own principles fairly and consistently. Let the same mode of ar-gument be adopted in all cases alike ; and then it can no longer be attributed to hostile prejudice, but to enlarged and philo-sophical views. If they have already rejected some histories, on the ground of their being strange and marvellous, — of their relating facts unprecedented and at variance with the estab-lished course of nature, — let them not give credit to another history which lies open to the very same objections, — the

---

[1] Germaniæ vocabulum recens et nuper additum; quoniam qui primi Rhe-num transgressi Gallos expulerint, ac nunc Tungri, tunc Germani vocati sint; ita nationis nomen in nomen gentis evaluisse paullatum, ut omnes, primum a victore ob metum, mox a seipsis invento nomine, Germani vocarentur.— *Tacit-tus, de Mor. Germ.*

4

extraordinary and romantic tale we have been just considering. If they have discredited the testimony of witnesses, who are *said* at least to have been disinterested, and to have braved persecutions and death in support of their assertions, can these philosophers consistently listen to and believe the testimony of those who avowedly *get money* by the tales they publish, and who do not even pretend that they incur any serious risk in case of being detected in a falsehood? If, in other cases, they have refused to listen to an account which has passed through many intermediate hands before it reaches them, and which is defended by those who have an interest in maintaining it, let them consider through how many, and what very suspicious hands, *this* story has arrived to them, without the possibility, as I have shown, of tracing it back to any decidedly authentic source, after all, — to any better authority, according to their own showing, than that of an *unnamed* and unknown foreign correspondent; and likewise how strong an interest, in every way, those who have hitherto imposed on them, have in keeping up the imposture. Let them, in short, show themselves as ready to detect the cheats and despise the fables of politicians as of priests.

But if they are still wedded to the popular belief in this point, let them be consistent enough to admit the same evidence in *other* cases which they yield to in *this*. If, after all that has been said, they cannot bring themselves to doubt of the existence of Napoleon Buonaparte, they must at least acknowledge that they do not apply to that question the same plan of reasoning which they have made use of in others; and they are consequently bound in reason and in honesty to re-nounce it altogether.

APPENDIX.

It may seem arrogant for an obscure and nameless individual to claim the glory of having put to death the most formidable of all recorded heroes. But a shadowy champion may be overthrown by a shadowy antagonist. Many a terrific spectre has been laid by the beams of a halfpenny candle. And if I have succeeded in making out, in the foregoing pages, a probable case of suspicion, it must, I think, be admitted, that there is some ground for my present boast of having *killed* Napoleon Buonaparte.

Let but the circumstances of the case be considered. This mighty emperor, who had been so long the bugbear of the civilized world, after having obtained successes and undergone reverses, such as never befel any (other at least) *real* potentate, was at length sentenced to confinement in the remote island of St. Helena,— a measure which many persons wondered at, and many objected to, on various grounds, not unreasonably supposing the illustrious exile to be a real person; but on the supposition of his being only a man of straw, the situation was exceedingly favorable for keeping him out of the way of impertinent curiosity, when not wanted, and for making him the foundation of any new plots that there might be occasion to conjure up.

About this juncture it was that the public attention was first invited by these pages, to the question as to the real existence of Napoleon Buonaparte. They excited, it may be fairly supposed, along with much surprise and much censure, some degree of doubt, and probably of consequent inquiry. No fresh evidence, as far as I can learn, of the truth of the disputed points, was brought forward to dispel these doubts. We heard, however, of the most jealous precautions being used to prevent any intercourse between the formidable prisoner and any stranger who, from motives of curiosity, might wish to visit him. The "man in the iron mask" could hardly have been more rigorously secluded; and we also heard various contradictory reports of conversations between him and the few who were allowed access to him; the falsehood and inconsistency of most of these reports being proved in contemporary publications.

At length, just about the time when the public scepticism respecting this extraordinary personage might be supposed to have risen to an alarming height, it was announced to us that he was dead! A stop was thus put, most opportunely, to all troublesome inquiries. I do not undertake to deny that such a person did live and die. That he was, and that he did, *everything* that is reported, we cannot believe, unless we consent to admit contradictory statements; but many of the events recorded, however marvellous, are certainly not, when taken separately, physically impossible. But I would only entreat the candid reader to reflect what might naturally be expected, on the supposition of the surmises contained in the present work being well founded. Supposing the whole of the tale I have been considering to have been a fabrication, what would be the natural result of such an attempt to excite inquiry into its truth? Evidently the shortest and most effectual mode of eluding detection, would be to *kill* the phantom, and so get rid of him at once. A ready and decisive answer would thus be provided to any one in whom the foregoing arguments might have excited suspicions, — "Sir, there can be no doubt that such a person existed, and performed what is related of him; and if you will just take a voyage to St. Helena, you may see with your own eyes, — not him, indeed, for he is no longer living, — but his *tomb;* and what evidence would you have that is more decisive?"

So much for his *death:* as for his *life,* it is just published by an eminent writer; besides which, the shops will
supply us with abundance of busts and prints of this great man;
all striking likenesses — of one another. The most incredulous
must be satisfied with this! "Stat magni NOMINIS umbra!"

KONX OMPAX.

POSTSCRIPT TO THE SEVENTH EDITION.

SINCE the publication of the Sixth Edition of this work, the
French nation, and the world at large, have obtained an additional evidence, to which I hope they will attach as much
weight as it deserves, of the reality of the wonderful history I
have been treating of. ·The great nation, among the many
indications lately given of an heroic zeal like what Homer at-
tributes to his Argive warriors, τίσασϑαι ʽΕΛΕʹΝΗΣ ὁρμή-
ματά τε στοναχάς τε, have formed and executed the design
of bringing home for honorable interment the remains of their
illustrious chief.

How many persons have actually inspected these relics, I
have not ascertained; but that a real coffin, containing real
bones, was brought from St. Helena to France, I see no reason
to disbelieve.

Whether future visitors to St. Helena will be shown merely
the identical *place* in which Buonaparte was (*said* to have been)
interred, or whether another set of real bones will be exhibited
in that island, we have yet to learn.

This latter supposition is not very improbable. It was
something of a credit to the island, an attraction to strangers,
and a source of profit to some or the inhabitants, to possess so
remarkable a relic; and this glory and advantage they must
naturally wish to retain. If so, there seems no reason why

4*

they should not have a Buonaparte of their own; for there is, I believe, no doubt that there are, or were, several museums in England, which, among other curiosities, boasted, each, of a genuine skull of Oliver Cromwell.

Perhaps, therefore, we shall hear of several well-authenticated skulls of Buonaparte also, in the collections of different virtuosos, all of whom (especially those in whose own crania the "organ of wonder" is the most largely developed), will doubtless derive equal satisfaction from the relics they respectively possess.

POSTSCRIPT TO THE NINTH EDITION.

THE public has been of late much interested, and not a little bewildered, by the accounts of many strange events, said to have recently taken place in France and other parts of the Continent. Are these accounts of such a character as to allay, or to strengthen and increase, such doubts as have been suggested in the foregoing pages?

We are told that there is now a Napoleon Buonaparte at the head of the government of France. It is not, indeed, asserted that he is the very original Napoleon Buonaparte himself. The death of that personage, and the transportation of his genuine bones to France, had been too widely proclaimed to allow of his reappearance in his own proper person. But "uno avulso, non deficit alter." Like the Thibetian worshippers of the Delai Lama (who never dies; only, his soul transmigrates into a fresh body), the French are so resolved, we are told, to be under a Buonaparte — whether that be (see note to p. 36) a man or "a system"— that they have found, it seems, a kind of new incarnation of this their grand Lama, in a person said to be the nephew of the original one.

And when, on hearing that this personage now fills the high office of President of the French Republic, we inquire (very naturally) *how he came there*, we are informed that, several years ago, he invaded France in an English vessel (the *Engglish* — as was observed in p. 34 — having always been suspected of keeping Buonaparte ready, like the winds in a Lapland witch's bag, to be let out on occasion), at the head of a force, not of six hundred men, like his supposed uncle in his expedition from Elba, but of fifty-five (!), with which he landed at Boulogne, proclaimed himself emperor, and was joined by no less than *one* man! He was accordingly, we are told, arrested, brought to trial, and sentenced to imprisonment; but having, some years after, escaped from prison, and taken refuge in England (*England* again!), he thence returned to France; AND so the French nation placed him at the head of the government!

All this will doubtless be received as a very probable tale, by those who have given full credit to all the stories I have alluded to in the foregoing pages.

POSTSCRIPT TO THE ELEVENTH EDITION.

WHEN any dramatic piece *takes* — as the phrase is — with the public, it will usually be represented again and again with still-continued applause; and sometimes imitations of it will be produced; so that the same drama in substance will, with occasional slight variations in the plot, and changes of names, long keep possession of the stage.

Something like this has taken place with respect to that curious tragi-comedy — the scene of it laid in France — which has engaged the attention of the British public for about sixty years; during which it has been "exhibited to crowded houses" —namely, coffee-houses, reading-rooms, etc.—with unabated interest.

The outline of this drama, or series of dramas, may be thus sketched:

DRAMATIS PERSONÆ.

A.—A King or other Sovereign.

B.—His Queen.

C.—The Heir apparent.

D. E. F.—His Ministers.

G. H. I. J. K.—Demagogues.

L.—A popular leader, of superior ingenuity, who becomes ultimately supreme ruler, under the title of Dictator, Consul, Emperor, King, President, or some other.

Soldiers, Senators, Executioners, and other functionaries, Citizens, Fishwomen, etc.

Scene, Paris.

I. The first Act of one of these dramas represents a monarchy, somewhat troubled by murmurs of disaffection, suspicions of conspiracy, etc.

II. Second Act, a rebellion; in which ultimately the government is overthrown.

III. Act the third, a provisional government established, on principles of liberty, equality, fraternity, etc.

IV. Act the fourth, struggles of various parties for power, carried on with sundry intrigues and sanguinary conflicts.

V. Act the fifth, the reestablishment of some form of absolute monarchy.

And from this point we start afresh, and begin the same business over again, with sundry fresh interludes.

All this is highly amusing to the English public to *hear* and *read* of; but I doubt whether our countrymen would like to be actual *performers* in such a drama.

Whether the French really are so, or whether they are mystifying us in the accounts they send over, I will not presume to decide. But if the former supposition be the true one, — if they have been so long really acting over and over again in their own persons such a drama, it must be allowed that they deserve to be characterized as they have been in the description given of certain European nations, — "An Englishman," it has been said, "is never happy but when he is miserable; a Scotchman is never at home but when he is abroad; an Irishman is never at peace but when he is fighting; a Spaniard is never at liberty but when he is enslaved; and a Frenchman is never settled but when he is engaged in a revolution."

Besides the many strange and improbable circumstances in the history of Buonaparte that have been noticed in the foregoing pages, there are many others that have been omitted, two of which it may be worth while to advert to.

One of the most incredible is the received account of the persons known as the "Detenus." It is well known that a great number of English gentlemen passed many years, in the early part of the present century, abroad, — by their own account, in France. Their statement was, that, while travelling in that country for their amusement, as peaceable tourists, they were, on the sudden breaking out of a war, seized by this terrible Buonaparte, and kept prisoners for about twelve years, contrary to all the usages of civilized nations, — to all principles of justice, of humanity, of enlightened policy; many of them thus wasting in captivity the most important portion of their lives, and having all their prospects blighted.

Now, whether these persons were in reality exiles by choice, for the sake of keeping out of the way of creditors, or of enjoying the society of those they preferred to their own domestic circle, I do not venture to conjecture. But let the reader consider whether *any* conjecture can be *more* improbable than the statement actually made.

It is, indeed, credible that ambition may prompt an unscrupulous man to make the most enormous sacrifices of human life, and to perpetrate the most atrocious crimes, for the advancement of his views of conquest. But that this *great* man — as he is usually reckoned even by adversaries — this hero according to some — this illustrious warrior and mighty sovereign — should have stooped to be guilty of an act of mean and petty malice worthy of a spiteful old woman, — a piece of paltry cruelty which could not at all conduce to his success in the war, or produce any effect except to degrade his country, and exasperate ours, — this, surely, is quite incredible. "Pizarro," says Elvira, in Kotzebue's play, "if not always justly, at least act always greatly."

But a still more wonderful circumstance connected with this transaction remains behind. A large portion of the English nation, and among these the whole of the Whig party, are said to have expressed the most vehement indignation, mingled with compassion, at the banishment from Europe, and confinement in St. Helena, of this great man. No considerations of regard for the peace and security of our own country, no dread of the power of so able and indefatigable a warrior, and so inveterate an enemy, should have induced us, they thought, to subject this formidable personage to a confinement which was far less severe than that to which he was said to have subjected such numbers of our countrymen, the harmless, *non-belligerent* travellers, whom (according to the story) he kidnapped in France, with no object but to gratify the basest and most unmanly spite.

But there is no truth in that story; and that it was not believed by those who manifested so much sympathy and indignation on this great man's account, is sufficiently proved by that very sympathy and indignation.

There are, again, other striking improbabilities connected with the Polish nation in the history before us. Buonaparte is represented as having always expressed the strongest sympathy with that ill-used people; and they, as being devotedly attached to him, and fighting with the utmost fidelity and bravery in his armies, in which some of them obtained high commands. Now he had it manifestly in his power at one period (according to the received accounts), with a stroke

of his pen to reëstablish Poland as an independent state.
For, in his last Russian war, he had complete occupation of
the country (of which the population was perfectly friendly);
the Russian portion of it was his by right of conquest;
and Austria and Prussia, then his allies, and almost his sub-
jects, would gladly have resigned their portions in exchange
for some of the provinces they had ceded to France, and which
were, to him, of little value, but, to them, important. And,
indeed, Prussia was (as we are told) so thoroughly humbled
and weakened, that he might easily have enforced the cession
of Prussian-Poland, even without any compensation. And
the reëstablishment of the Polish kingdom would have been as
evidently politic as it was reasonable. The independence of
a faithful and devoted ally, at enmity with the surrounding
nations — the very nations that were the most likely to combine (as they often had done) against him, — this would have
given him, at no cost, a kind of strong garrison to maintain his
power, and to keep his enemies in check.

Yet this most obvious step, the history tells us, he did not
take; but made flattering speeches to the Poles, used their
services, and did nothing for them!

This is, alone, sufficiently improbable. But we are required,
moreover, to believe that the Poles, instead of *execrating*
this man who had done them the unpardonable wrong of wantonly disappointing the expectations he had, for his purposes,
excited, thus adding treachery to ingratitude, — instead of this,
continued to the last as much devoted to him as ever, and even
now idolize his memory! We are to believe, in short, that
this Buonaparte, not only in his own conduct and adventures
violated all the established rules' of probability, but also caused
all other persons, as many as came in contact with him, to act
as no mortals ever did act before: may we not add, as no mortals ever did act at all?

Many other improbabilities might be added to the list, and
will be found in the complete edition of that history, from
which some extracts have been given in the foregoing pages,

and which has been published (under the title of "Historic certainties") by Aristarchus Newlight, with a learned commentary (not, indeed, adopting the views contained in the foregoing pages, but) quite equal in ingenuity to a late work on the "Hebrew Monarchy."